POKÉMON™
THE SERIES

SUN & MOON

The Great Pancake Race

Adapted by Jeanette Lane

©2018 The Pokémon Company International. ©1997-2018 Nintendo, Creatures, GAME FREAK, TV Tokyo, ShoPro, JR Kikaku. TM, ® Nintendo.

Published by Scholastic Inc., *Publishers since 1920*. SCHOLASTIC and associated logos are trademarks and/or registered trademarks of Scholastic Inc.

ISBN 978-1-338-19366-4

12 11 10 9 8 7 6 5 4 3 2   18 19 20 21 22

Printed in the U.S.A.   40

First printing 2018

SCHOLASTIC INC.

"What is Bounsweet up to?" Rotom Dex asked Ash.

Ash wondered, too. He watched his friend Mallow's Bounsweet bounce back and forth.

"Beats me," Ash replied. "Mallow? What's going on?"

"Not now," Mallow said. "We're working!"

Ash, Pikachu, and Rotom Dex were studying at the Pokémon School in Alola. Mallow and Bounsweet were students there, too.

"That's the spirit!" Mallow called to Bounsweet. "If we keep training for the race, you'll get even faster!"

"Did you say 'race'?" Ash asked.

"That's right," Mallow replied. "The Pokémon Pancake Race is an island tradition."

The next day, Ash and Professor Kukui
went out to eat.
Pikachu and Rockruff went, too.
At the restaurant, they met Nina and Raichu.

"Nina and Raichu won the Pokémon Pancake Race last year," Professor Kukui told Ash.

"I can see why you're the champion," Ash said to Raichu. "The way you float is so cool!"

"If the pancakes fall or you drop your plate, you're out," Nina told Ash. "But it's so much fun!"

"Do you want to enter the race?" Ash asked Pikachu.

"*Pika pika!*" Pikachu agreed.

The next day, everyone started training.
Nina and Raichu helped Ash and Pikachu.
After practice, Pikachu was very tired.
"You gave it your all," Ash said.

Team Rocket was spying on Ash and Pikachu.

Meowth read a poster about the race.

Jessie wanted to win the prize.

It was a year of free pancakes. Yum!

The day of the race finally arrived.
The announcer told the Trainers and
their Pokémon partners about the course.
The Trainers would go first.

The Trainers went to the starting line.
Principal Oak, Ash, and his classmates
were all there.

"When it comes to teamwork, Pikachu and
I can't be beat!" Ash said.

"Ready, set, go!" yelled the announcer.

The Trainers had to climb steep hills.
They had to walk on balance beams.
They tried to hold the pancakes nice and
steady.

Anyone who dropped a pancake was out of the race.

Sophocles tripped early. "Oh no!" he cried.

In the next stage of the race, the Trainers
had to pull their Pokémon in wagons.
Ash and Pikachu were moving fast.

Kiawe was very strong, but Turtonator was
very heavy!

Principal Oak's partner was a Komala, the Drowsing Pokémon.

Komala was always asleep—even when it was racing!

Zzzzzzz!

Jessie's partner was Mimikyu. She
tugged the wagon with all her might.
"I won't stop until I pop!" she cried.
Jessie really wanted to win the pancakes!

James was racing with Bewear, but it wasn't a *real* Bewear. It was a robot in a Bewear costume.

Meowth and Wobbuffet were hiding inside.

"My Robo Racer Pancake Chaser is the best!" Meowth bragged.

Finally, it was the last stage of the race.
Only the Pokémon were racing now.
Raichu was in the lead.
Pikachu was second!

Mimikyu was catching up. It aimed a
Shadow Ball at Pikachu. But it was against
the rules to use attacks.

Tricky Mimikyu was kicked out of the race!

Raichu floated along. It held the pancake plate in one hand.
Raichu made the race look easy.

Pikachu would not give up.
"*Pika, pika, pika!*" it panted.
The plate of pancakes rested on its back.
The race was hard work!

Raichu bounded ahead.
Pikachu gritted its teeth.
It ran harder.

The Trainers all watched and cheered.
"Go for it, Pikachu!" Ash yelled.
"All right!" Nina called out. "Pikachu's
turned this into a real race!"

Bewear and Komala were still in the race, too. They were not far behind.

The finish line was getting close!

Meowth and Wobbuffet were still inside
the Bewear costume.
"Let's give it some gas," Meowth said.
Meowth put the robot in high gear.
The rockets fired up.

The Bewear robot sped forward.

"Don't blow your stack," Meowth said.

But the robot went faster and faster.

"My Robo Racer's going nuts!" Meowth cried.

The Bewear robot whizzed past Raichu and Pikachu.

It crossed the finish line first.

"Free pancakes for a year!" Jessie cheered.

But then the *real* Bewear appeared.

The real Bewear tackled the Bewear robot.

The costume flew off.

Meowth and Wobbuffet tumbled into the air.

"The lead racer was a fake Pokémon!" the announcer said.

No robots were allowed in the race!
The Bewear robot was kicked out.
The real Bewear grabbed Team Rocket
and ran away.
"Oh no, not again," Jessie, James, and
Meowth groaned.

Pikachu and Raichu stopped to watch.
But Komala kept rolling.
Komala rolled right past them!

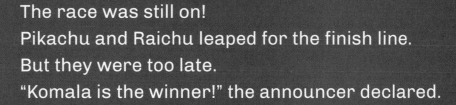

The race was still on!
Pikachu and Raichu leaped for the finish line.
But they were too late.
"Komala is the winner!" the announcer declared.

Pikachu and Raichu tied for second place.

"You were really amazing out there," Ash told his best friend.

The Pokémon Pancake Race was a great tradition.

And our heroes are always ready for their next adventure!